# MAX AND KATIE'S
# AZTEC ADVENTURE

BY SAMANTHA METCALF

ILLUSTRATED BY IAN R. WARD

Published in Great Britain in 2016 by:
Mysteries in Time Limited
info@mysteriesintime.co.uk

Illustrated by Ian R. Ward.
www.ianrward.co.uk

A catalogue record for this book is available from the British Library.

ISBN 978-0-9935660-5-9

Hi! I'm Katie and I am 8 years old. Max is my older brother. He's really clever. He helps me with my home work when I'm stuck. He knows everything! But don't tell him I said that. He can get really annoying and know-it-all. He is always telling me stuff, but sometimes it's just too much. All I want is a simple answer, like 'yes' or 'no'. Instead, it's always 'maybe, because...' So annoying.

But he's not so bad. He always looks out for me. And we have fun playing games together.

I think my favourite thing is playing outside in any weather! I love going to the park, especially the adventure playground with the huge, curly slide. You can go really fast on that one, especially when you lie down! Mum hates it when I come home covered in mud, but I can't help it. The fun parts of the park are always the muddiest.

Hey, I'm Max and I'm 11. I love reading. I read comics and cartoons that make me laugh, and I read adventure stories about knights and castles, or pirates and buried treasure! Mum is always telling me I have an overactive imagination. I can't help it. My mind just starts picturing loads of weird stuff.

I also love solving puzzles. Grandpa always buys me books full of word-searches and crosswords. I like to time myself and see how fast I can solve them.

Katie is my younger sister. She is really energetic and fun to be around. She's really fast and sporty. I wish I could be as good as her at sports. But don't tell her I said that. She can also be really annoying, when she can't sit still for more than five minutes. And she doesn't stop talking!

But she's cool. I'm pleased she's my sister.

# 1

Katie was being unusually quiet. It was Saturday morning and normally she would have been in all sorts of trouble by now. Max was suspicious. He went to find her.

Katie was curled up on her bed with her eyes shut tight.

"Are you asleep?" he asked.

"Yes," answered Katie sarcastically. "What a silly thing to ask!" Katie's eyes opened and she quickly sat up straight.

"Well, it's not really that silly, because your eyes were closed!" answered Max.

"But if I were asleep, then I couldn't answer!" laughed Katie. "You should ask if I'm awake!"

Max shrugged his shoulders. She was right, but he wasn't going to admit it.

"But why are you pretending to sleep? Don't you

realise your favourite cartoon has started?"

Katie looked very serious. She tiptoed to her bedroom door and listened carefully. She gently closed it. "Mum says I have to go to the hairdresser today. But I hate having my hair cut," she said with wide eyes. "It's sooooo boring!"

Max understood. Katie was rubbish at sitting still for longer than five minutes. She was too impatient.

"So you're hiding here and hoping that Mum forgets?!" laughed Max. "You'll have to go at some point! You don't want to become one of those people who carry their hair like a scarf so they don't trip up over it!"

Katie was busy imagining what this would feel like, when they heard the doorbell.

Max and Katie looked at each other in excitement.

"You wait here," said Max. "If it is another adventure, I don't want to have to wait for you to come back from the hairdresser either!"

Katie listened at the door. She heard Max bounce down the stairs... then stop... the door opened... Mum's voice... someone outside... the door closed...

Max bounded up the stairs two at a time, then burst into the room with a turquoise adventure in his hands.

"Quick," whispered Katie. "Where will we go this

time?"

They opened the box and found the Mission Plan.

# Mission Plan

Place:          Tenochtitlan
Date:           January 1519


Tenochtitlan was the capital city of the
Aztec Empire.

Meztli, a thirteen-year-old boy, has been a
slave for  six years. He has been sold twice,
and is about to be sold for a third time.
This means he can be sent to be sacrificed.
His only hope is to escape.

Aztec law says that slaves will be freed
if they can run all the way to the palace
without being caught by their owner. Nobody
is allowed to help either the slave or the
owner, or their life will also be in danger.


Task:

Can you help this slave run to his freedom,
without getting caught yourself?

# 2

"Slaves? Sacrifices?" Katie gulped noisily. "This sounds like the most dangerous mission yet."

Max agreed.

They read the history booklet to learn as much as they could that might help them. They learnt that thousands of people - including children - were sacrificed by the Aztecs each year.

"Apparently it was a great honour to be sacrificed!" shrieked Katie.

"Shhhh," whispered Max. "Would you prefer the hairdresser?"

Katie threw her hands in the air. "Yes! I think even *I* think that having my hair trimmed is a little better than having my heart cut out and eaten!"

Max ignored her sarcasm and continued reading. He read about slaves, chocolate, gods and temples.

"They had pyramids and hieroglyphs," he said,

trying to distract his sister from the danger they were facing. "Similar to the Ancient Egyptians. And they loved hot chocolate!"

But Katie was doing an impressive job of ignoring him.

"We are going to travel back to the year 1519," he continued. "That's the same year that the Spanish arrived and the Aztecs thought Hernan Cortes was the god, Quetzalcoatl! At least we are going before they arrive."

Max found the Time Travel Sticker. This time it was a simple bird symbol.

"This bird symbolises strength and courage," explained Max.

"Good," said Katie grumpily. "We'll need all the help we can get on this mission."

Katie only cheered up when she saw what clothes the Aztecs wore. Soon, she was rolling on the floor in laughter, clutching her tummy.

"What's so funny?" asked Max innocently.

"You... you..." wheezed Katie. "You have to wear a nappy!" she finally said. "At least I get to wear normal clothes!"

"Er, I think they're more like shorts." But Max had gone pale.

Katie was right.

Boys didn't wear very much in the Aztec world.

# 3

Max and Katie decided to see if they could make their clothes themselves. Max had a plain white t-shirt that was quite long on Katie.

She used a red and yellow pen to carefully draw a pattern around the bottom of the t-shirt and around the sleeves and collar.

They found some white bed sheets in the cupboard and Katie cut and sewed two ends together to make a long skirt. She then added the same geometric pattern to the hem of the skirt.

Katie added the same pattern to the edge of another sheet, which Max turned into a cloak by tying two corners into a knot over his shoulder.

The only thing left to make was Max's shorts.

Max trimmed a bed sheet so it looked like a very long strip of material. He wrapped this around his body so his shorts were completely covered. He looked just like the Aztecs in the pictures, but he still looked worried.

"It's fine," said Katie. "Don't worry! Everyone will be wearing the same thing!"

"Do you remember when it was non-uniform day last year and we went into school wearing our own clothes?" asked Max. "Remember how I got the day wrong and turned up in my own clothes while

everyone else had their uniform on?" Max shuddered at the memory. "Sooo embarrassing!"

Katie shook her head. "This is nothing like that time. We know what everyone will be wearing. Besides, you have the cloak to wrap around yourself if you feel uncomfortable."

Max had an idea. He quickly gathered some clothes together and put them in a bag. "Just in case," he explained.

Katie nodded.

"Ready!" they agreed.

# 4

It was time to go.

With his bag firmly in his left hand, Max programmed the time machine and pushed the big red button with his right hand.

There was a low humming sound that got increasingly louder. At the same time, the room started to spin around them, getting faster and faster. Max and Katie closed their eyes to stop themselves getting too dizzy.

It wasn't long before they felt the ground steady beneath their feet and the warm glow of the sun on their faces. Max shaded his eyes with his hand and looked around. Katie squinted at the busy market place where they had landed.

It felt like a bustling city with people everywhere. There were market stalls selling different kinds of vegetables and exotic fruit.

They could see simple boats moving slowly through the canals, carrying maize to the market.

Max was relieved, because all men and boys were wearing the same thing, some even without the cloak!

He understood now: it was too hot to wear much else!

At the furthest end of the large paved square was an enormous pyramid. It was different to the pyramids they had seen in Egypt. This one was built with different platforms, each one smaller than the one below, creating a pyramid shape. There were steps leading up to the temple at the very top.

It cast a shadow over the people going about their business in the market below.

Max's eyes were drawn to the market. He could see a man wearing a tall headdress made from feathers. Max realised that he must be very wealthy, because he also wore gold bracelets.

Trying to see what this man was selling, Max went onto his tip-toes. It wasn't long before he realised he wasn't selling fruit or vegetables or even animals.

He was selling people. People with wooden blocks around their necks.

These were the slaves.

# 5

"We have to find Meztli," said Max. "Come on!"

Katie followed Max as they weaved in and out of people. They reached the place where slaves were being paraded around.

"How will we know it's him?" asked Katie in despair. "There are hundreds of people here!"

Just then, there was a loud commotion nearby. People started shrieking and rushing out of the way. Katie was shorter than everyone around her, so she couldn't see what was going on.

"Watch out!" yelled Max suddenly.

She spun around and saw a slave running straight at her. He was looking over his shoulder to see if he was being chased, so he didn't see Katie. The wooden block was in line to hit Katie square on the forehead.

She threw her hands up to her face and shut her eyes tight, waiting for the impact.

# 6

The impact never came.

Instead, Katie felt herself flying through the air.

She landed on something soft and opened her eyes.

Someone had pulled her out of harm's way just in time! She had landed on a pile of maize ready for sale at the market.

Katie stood up, brushed her hair out of her eyes

and looked at the person who had saved her.

"Thank you!" she said to a boy with a wooden block around his neck. "What happened?"

The boy smiled. "That was a slave making a run for the palace. If he makes it there without being caught, he will win his freedom."

Max was standing next to her. They both looked at each other. They were both thinking the same thing: had they missed their chance to help Meztli? Were they too late?

Max introduced himself and Katie.

"Nice to meet you," replied the boy. "My name's Meztli."

Max and Katie couldn't believe their luck! This was the boy they were here to help!

"Come on," said Meztli. "Let's see if he made it!"

Max and Katie followed him to the steps of the nearby pyramid and climbed up so they could see the whole scene. They could see his head bobbing up and down as he ran through the crowd, far in the distance.

"Who's chasing him?" asked Katie.

"Only the owner or the owner's son is allowed to chase a slave who is running for his freedom," explained Meztli. "There are many rules. Nobody is allowed to help either the slave or the chaser. If they do, then they too will become slaves."

They watched the runaway slave race through the busy market. It looked like the chaser was about to catch him, but suddenly the path opened up in front of the boy, who picked up speed as fast as he could.

He made it! He was inside the palace. Several people nearby cheered.

"He is free! He is very lucky," said Meztli.

Max saw his chance. "Maybe you should also run for your freedom."

Meztli smiled and shook his head. "I would like to, but now that he has raced and won, all owners

18

will be watching us carefully, expecting us to run too."

Katie looked around to check nobody was listening.

"We would help you," she whispered. "We owe you for saving my life back there."

"I think you're exaggerating a little! Your life wasn't in danger." smiled Meztli. "Come on, it's lunch time. I have to cook for my master, but there are always leftovers."

Max and Katie followed Meztli to his master's house. They caught a glimpse of his master through the door. Max realised it was the same man he had seen in the market! He wore a brightly-coloured cloak, golden bracelets and a headdress made of blue and red feathers.

Max and Katie hid at the back of the kitchen, out of sight. After the master had eaten, Meztli brought over some tortillas made from maize and some delicious cooked vegetables. They ate with their hands. As they ate, they talked quietly.

"We will help you," promised Max, "but me and Katie are only in town for one day. Today is the only chance we have to help you."

Meztli checked over his shoulder. "But all the masters will be watching us like hawks today, because that other slave ran for his freedom."

"Then we have to be especially sneaky," said Max.

They decided to make sure the coast was clear for Meztli to run as fast as he could, but then somehow cause a crowd to gather behind him, blocking the chaser and slowing him down. This would give Meztli a better chance at making it to the palace.

"But how?" asked Katie. "What would make everyone scatter at the same time?"

"And then make them gather together again straight away," finished Meztli.

Max suddenly sat up straight. "I have an idea."

# 7

Meztli carried out his usual afternoon duties, under the watchful eye of his master.

"He knows, I'm sure he knows!" hissed Meztli when he saw Max in the kitchen again.

"No, you're just being paranoid," answered Max. "Don't worry, stick to the plan and you'll be free in just a few hours!"

Soon, it was time. Max and Katie set off ahead. On the way, Max explained his plan.

"You can run faster than me," explained Max. "You'll be able to catch up with Meztli wherever he is no problem. So you should be the back-up."

"Back-up for what?" asked Katie.

"Back-up for me," gulped Max. "In case I get caught."

"But... but... but what will happen to you if you get caught?"

"Don't worry. They will just make me a slave," explained Max. "It won't matter, because when we're done, I will just transport back to the modern day with you!"

Katie thought about this and realised he was right. Well, she hoped he was right.

"And what will you do?" she asked.

Max explained that he was going to wait near the beginning of the route, close to Meztli's master's house. His first job was to slow down the Master.

"I will spread the rumour that the great god, Quetzalcoatl, is arriving today," explained Max.

"How on earth will that help Meztli?"

"I'll tell them that he will be angry if this slave is not freed, that one day Meztli will become the most important emperor this civilisation has ever seen. That they are destined to worship him."

"What if they don't believe you?" asked Katie.

"They have to."

# 8

Meanwhile, Meztli waited for his best chance. His master was getting ready to take him to the market.

Meztli had hidden his master's favourite headdress, as planned.

"Go find it, you idiot!" yelled his master.

Meztli bowed his head and left the room. This was his chance. He checked he wasn't being watched and started running. He ran as fast as he possibly could. He didn't dare to look round.

He made it round the first corner and out into the open.

His heart dropped.

The road was blocked!

There were two people having an argument and a crowd had formed round them. This was definitely not part of the plan! He could feel himself starting to panic. He took a few deep breaths and looked round. He saw Max waving frantically to him from beside the nearest temple. He must know a way through!

Meztli quickly set off again at a sprint in the new direction. He knew he had lost precious minutes and his master could be close on his heels by now.

Max disappeared round the corner of the small temple. For a split second, Meztli worried that he didn't know these two strangers with foreign-sounding names and fair hair. Why on earth had he agreed to trust them? The risk of getting caught was high; the punishment would be worse.

It would definitely be sacrifice this time.

He felt sick at the thought.

"Well," he told himself. "Just don't get caught!"

He rounded the corner of the temple just in time to see Max's back turn the next corner. He pushed himself harder, faster.

He was now back on the main street. He had got past the first crowd, but there was nothing stopping his master from doing the same behind him.

Up ahead, he saw a second crowd was gathered. Was this part of the plan, or just another accident or argument? Would the plan even work? Doubt after doubt passed through Meztli's mind.

He slowed a little, unsure whether Max would be true to his word.

He stopped in front of the crowd of people.

"There's no hope now!" he cried in despair, throwing his hands up to his face.

Suddenly the crowd stopped and stared at him.

His heart was beating extra fast. He was looking at a wall of faces. Nobody was moving. His path was blocked.

"Is it him?" asked a lady at the front.

"It must be him!" exclaimed her friend.

"That strange-looking boy was right," replied a

man next to her. "That must mean that the mighty Quetzalcoatl is on his way!"

Just when Meztli thought nothing would happen, the crowd started to move.

"Get out of his way!" shouted another. "We mustn't anger the gods!"

Meztli couldn't believe his eyes. The crowd was actually moving apart.

Meztli looked behind him, and spotted his master coming round the corner of the temple.

Now! He had to run now!

Meztli started running towards the gap. The crowd was watching him as he ran past. They all turned as he ran, not taking their eyes off him.

Max's plan was working!

He even dared to look over his shoulder to check if the crowd closed the gap behind him as well.

He couldn't believe his eyes! Every single person stepped closer together. There was no way through!

He could see the top of his master's headdress at the back, trying to push his way through the crowd.

Meztli could see the end in sight! He ran as fast as he could and practically fell over the finish line and into the palace!

# 9

Meztli was on his knees, desperately catching his breath when he realised he was being watched. His eyes slowly lifted to take in the two feet in front of him. He noticed the beautifully carved chair that this person was sitting on. It wasn't like an ordinary chair. It was definitely much grander than anything his master ever sat on.

In fact, it was more like a throne.

He gulped.

He looked up and up, taking in everything that this man was wearing. His eyes were drawn to the most beautiful colours he had ever seen. A stunning headdress made from the long tail feathers of a quetzal bird. Rare feathers. They were shimmering turquoise, then green, then blue in the light.

His attention was pulled very quickly to the face of the great man in front of him. It was the Emperor.

"Congratulations," said the Emperor. "You have made the journey without being caught, so you are now free." He signalled to his guards to unlock the wooden neck brace.

Meztli was tongue-tied. He never thought he would get star-struck! His mouth was dry. All he could do was bow his head.

"Th-th-thank you," he eventually stammered.

Once released, Meztli left quietly and stepped outside into the sunshine. He was busy stretching his newly-released neck from side to side when Katie arrived and ran up to him, laughing.

"You did it!" she laughed. "You have won your freedom!"

Meztli laughed with her.

"It feels like a dream!" he cried.

But they didn't celebrate for long, because at that moment they heard an angrily frantic yell from the crowded market place. "Leave me alone!"

They couldn't see the owner of the voice. Katie didn't need to see it.

Katie recognised the voice.

It was Max.

# 10

Max had been making his way to the palace to meet Meztli, when he felt someone grab his arm.

He turned to face whoever this was, and came face-to-face with a wild cat's jaws. He was looking straight at the sharp teeth of a jaguar.

Terrified and confused, Max stumbled back. He looked again and realised it was a man with a hat on. A jaguar's head as a hat. The man's face was peering out from between the cat's jaws.

Max was dragged across the market square and up to the palace.

Katie and Meztli were standing still, watching. They felt helpless.

Katie was about to shout out, but Max gave her a warning look. Katie understood and kept silent.

Max was dragged to the Emperor.

"This is a traitor," explained the jaguar warrior.

"He must have been sent by our enemies, the Texlacans. He was found spreading rumours in the market place, probably to cause a public scare. His tribe's warriors are probably just outside our great city, waiting to attack."

The Emperor looked at Max with sparkling eyes. "Is this true?"

Max shook his head. He knew he had to sound strong. He gulped and tried to steady his nerves.

"No, of course it's not true," he replied. "I was

simply telling the truth. The great and mighty Quetzalcoatl is on his way. And he is not happy."

The Emperor looked worried for a moment as he watched Max's face. His eyes flickered around the room and he realised everyone was waiting for him to reply.

"Well, if that's true, then I know there is only one thing that will make our mighty god happy."

The crowd erupted into a loud cheer.

Katie smiled at Meztli. "Thank goodness!" she whispered. "For a minute there I thought Max was in trouble!"

But Meztli was not smiling. Katie looked from his pale face to Max, then to the Emperor.

"We shall have a special sacrifice at sunset today," he announced, standing up and leaving with his colourful cloak swirling in the breeze.

Max felt sick with shock.

This wasn't part of the plan.

# 11

Max was dragged onto his feet. He was once again staring into the jaws of an animal.

"Did you hear that?" snarled the man from inside the creature's jaws. "You are honoured to be the first sacrifice in front of the mighty Quetzalcoatl!"

Max's eyes glazed over from shock. He imagined it really was a walking, talking jaguar that had captured him. He felt dizzy.

Katie and Meztli watched Max be dragged off into the shadows.

She grabbed hold of Meztli's wrist and pulled him outside. They were standing in the blazing hot sun, but Katie was shaking.

"Wh-wh-what just happened?" she stuttered. "I should have said something, explained somehow."

"No," said Meztli. "If you had spoken up, then you would also be on your way to be sacrificed."

"But... but we have to save him!" cried Katie. "He's annoying and everything, but I don't want him to be sacrificed!"

They both sat down to think.

"The only way to save him, is if Quetzalcoatl really did turn up and ordered them to stop."

Katie sat up straight. "That's it!" she cried. "You're a genius!"

Meztli was shaking his head. "Er, I was only joking. If he did turn up, he would probably demand more sacrifices, not fewer!"

"Describe this god to me," urged Katie.

"Well, the prophecy says that he will arrive during a One Reed Year, wearing exotic clothes and with pale hair and a pale beard."

"This is a One Reed Year!" shrieked Katie. "That's why Max spread the rumour about that god. The prophecy says Quetzlcoatl will arrive this year! I have a plan. But hurry. It's not long until sunset."

# 12

Katie and Meztli ran back to the market place, where Max had hidden his bag earlier.

Meztli then ran to a friend's house to borrow a few items, including a knife and some beeswax.

They got to work.

Meztli cut off the ends of Katie's hair with the knife. He then used the beeswax to stick the hair cuttings to Katie's chin. She kept giggling because it

tickled.

"Hold still!" he laughed. "It has to set!"

Next, while the beeswax was drying, Meztli pulled out the different clothes that Max had brought with him from the future.

"What strange things you have," said Meztli quietly. "Are you sure you're not a god after all?"

Katie laughed and managed to dislodge a few strands of beard. "Oops," she replied and straightened her head carefully. She spoke without moving her mouth too much. "I am sure we are not gods. We just come from, er, very far away!"

She watched as Meztli held up a hooded top with a zip. She showed him how to make the zip work. His eyes widened at the pure magic that he was witnessing before his very eyes!

"It's cold where we come from," she explained.

He then pulled out a pair of sunglasses. Katie shrugged. "Cold but sunny."

Meztli was amazed by the effect when he held up the glasses to his eyes.

Meztli laughed. "It must be a very strange place."

Meztli stepped back and admired his creation.

Katie was wearing a hooded top, zipped up with the hood pulled up. She was wearing the sunglasses as well as a baseball cap with some beautiful turquoise feathers now attached.

She felt ridiculous, but remembered it was the only way to save Max.

The sun was starting to set.

It was time to go.

There wasn't much time.

# 13

Meanwhile, Max was being marched up the enormous stone steps to the top of the pyramid. He needed to looked down at his feet to watch his step, but froze.

There was a stain on each step.

A dark stain.

Like a river had once flowed and was now dried up.

A river of blood.

Max felt his knees go weak. Although he quite liked the idea of fainting right now, he realised his only hope of survival was to stay awake and alert.

He took lots of deep breaths and kept his eyes looking forward. He stayed strong, hoping that Katie had come up with a good plan.

# 14

Max  had now reached the top. He was looking
at an enormous stone altar. The Emperor was there
in his ceremonial clothes. Max concentrated his eyes
on the stunning feathers in the Emperor's enormous
headdress. The long quetzal feathers seemed to
change colour as they caught the light.

A priest was also there, with a cup of hot
chocolate and a ceremonial knife.

Max gulped.

"Do you have any final words, before this honour
is bestowed upon you?" boomed the priest.

Max had to think fast. "I wish you luck," he
started. "I wish you a swift end, when Quetzalcoatl
arrives and sees what you have done to me."

The priest's eye twitched. He looked uncertain.
He turned and looked at the Emperor.

"Continue!" yelled the Emperor. "We know what

will please him: the offer of your blood."

He waved his hand and Max was taken to the altar. He was held down and the crowd started to chant a prayer.

Just then, something caught the priest's eye.

"What on earth...?" he started.

Everyone followed his gaze.

# 15

There, stepping onto the top of the pyramid, was the strangest-looking creature they had ever seen.

"What is the meaning of this?" boomed an angry voice.

The priest shrank back in fear.

Max recognised his clothes! This creature was wearing his top, his sunglasses, even his baseball cap. But what on earth...?

Max peered closer. Could it be... Katie? Really? He felt his heart skip a beat. He was saved!

"Let him go!" ordered Katie, pointing at Max with a sharp spear decorated with feathers and the bright shoe laces from Max's trainers. "This boy warned you that I was arriving today. Why did you disobey me?"

Max thought she was starting to get a bit over-the-top now, but bit his tongue.

The Emperor gulped noisily then spoke.

"But, but, but we know that the blood of a sacrificed human is what pleases you! How has this changed?"

"I do NOT feed on BLOOD," roared Katie. "Now let him go!"

The jaguar warrior desperately untied Max and helped him up. He bowed to this god and stepped back.

Max was now close enough to Katie to see that

she was starting to sweat. Even though it was sunset, it was still very hot. And Katie was dressed for winter! His attention was drawn to Katie's chin. He could see the hairs stuck to her chin.

But the drops of sweat were rolling down Katie's cheek. Whatever she had used to glue the hairs to her chin was also starting to melt.

Her beard was slipping.

Her disguise would be discovered very soon.

They had to leave.

Now.

# 16

Max looked round at their escape route and realised just how high they had climbed. He could see for miles!

It was a shame he was currently in a life or death situation, because he would have loved a few minutes to admire the view.

The whole town was laid out below. He could

see the lake that surrounded the city; he could see the other temples around the edge of the square; he could see the network of canals all organised like a grid; he could even see Meztli's master's house in the distance and the route he had run.

It really was remarkable.

He turned back to the scene on the altar and saw the Emperor and the priest looking strangely at Katie.

"I have never liked the way you all sacrifice innocent people - especially children - and I command you to stop!" she ordered.

The jaguar warrior had taken a step closer.

"You will free all prisoners that were due to be sacrificed, or a great terror will hit your land." Katie was enjoying herself now.

Max gave her a little nudge and when he made eye contact with her, he looked meaningfully at her beard.

Katie understood, because she lowered her head and covered her chin with her hand.

"Yes, I believe you understand my wishes," she said and got ready to leave.

"Hey, wait!" called out the jaguar warrior. "Something's not right about you. Are you... melting?"

Katie gave a very loud, very false laugh. "No, and

get back! Do NOT come any closer."

Max and Katie stepped back.

Their heels were hanging off the edge of the stone step.

If they stepped back any further, they would fall.

They realised they had no escape route.

Any minute now, they would be pounced on. Katie's disguise would be discovered and there would be two sacrifices at sunset.

# 17

Just when Max and Katie were stepping dangerously close to the edge of the stone step, they felt something happen. There were sparks flying around them, gaining speed, like a tornado of fireflies.

They couldn't believe it. Surely not?! This never happened while they were in front of people!

They only just had the chance to see the shocked faces of the priest, the Emperor and the jaguar warrior, before the Aztec skies swirled around them. They felt the usual rush of time travel as well as the rush of relief that they were safe!

They landed back in Katie's bedroom.

They both realised they had both been holding their breath and gasped for air. They were shaking!

"Wow, that was close!" burst Katie. "I am very pleased the time travel gods brought us back in

time!"

"No!" groaned Max. "No more talk of gods!"

They got changed into their normal clothes and Katie cleaned off her fake beard.

"It's a shame we didn't get time to say goodbye to Meztli," said Katie. "He really did help us."

"That is a shame.," agreed Max. "But I also wish I could have seen all their faces after we disappeared into thin air!"

They both laughed at this thought.

"Do you think they will stop the sacrifices?" asked Katie seriously.

Max shrugged his shoulders. "I imagine they will stop for a while, but the Emperor will probably start it again as a way to control people with fear. Besides, the Spanish will appear soon, which will eventually lead to the end of the Aztecs, which means the end of sacrifices."

"Well, I hope we saved hundreds of lives at least," said Katie.

Max changed the subject. "Well, at least you don't need to visit the hairdressers any more!"

Katie brightened up. "True!"

"Hey, shall we get some hot chocolate?" suggested Max.

"Great idea," replied Katie, "Only I'll have mine without the sacrifice, thanks!"

The End.

See you on our next adventure!